*The Loves
of João Vêncio*

José Luandino Vieira

The Loves
of João Vêncio

Translated by
Richard Zenith

A Helen and Kurt Wolff Book
Harcourt Brace Jovanovich, Publishers
SAN DIEGO   NEW YORK   LONDON

HBJ

© 1979 by José Luandino Vieira—Edições 70
English translation copyright © 1991
by Harcourt Brace Jovanovich, Inc.

Library of Congress Cataloging-in-Publication Data
Vieira, José Luandino, 1935–
[João Vêncio, os seus amores. English]
The loves of João Vêncio / José Luandino Vieira : translated by
Richard Zenith. — 1st ed.
p. cm.
Translation of: João Vêncio, os seus amores.
"A Helen and Kurt Wolff book."
ISBN 0-15-146390-5
I. Title.
PQ9929.V54J613   1991
869.3—dc20   90-45618

Designed by Martha Roach
Printed in the United States of America
First edition
A B C D E

(just) for Linda

Translator's Note

The original edition of *The Loves of João Vêncio* states in a subtitle that the work is "an experiment in literary eloquence founded on slang, patois, and pimp terminology." It would be inappropriate to apply this epithet to my translation, in which the author's linguistic amalgam is not so apparent. The original text includes a sizable proportion of phrases in Kimbundu, a Bantu language of Angola, and provides an extensive glossary to aid the reader. I have chosen to make the entire text read in English, believing that it would be a greater infidelity to mix English together with Kimbundu, which in the voice of the narrator (and many Angolans) is not spoken as a purely separate language but forms a kind of hybrid with Portuguese. The book's Creole and slang terms likewise contribute to its linguistic complexity, and English-language equivalents must necessarily be specious, since they have no organic relation to the cultural reality of Angola. On the other hand, the narrator's personal penchant for deforming and re-forming language is to a large extent mirrored in the translation.

I thank Maria Manuela Rocha, Fernando Luís Machado, and the author himself, José Luandino Vieira, for helping to clarify doubtful terms.

Richard Zenith

*T*his man ask the craziest questions! . . . You want to know why I'm in the lockup? . . . It was my loves, my luck, it's life. . . . Too much rambling, too much rowdiness. And you? There—caught you! . . . Father Viêra taught me that trick: you get a question, you shoot one back. I like you, man, I don't mind your question. You'd know if I did. When I get stepped on I don't shout, I bite. Bush viper, that's what the prosecutor called me. I'd like to tell you my story for the record. I need your water. My thirst—you read me?— is ignorance. . . .

  You have a basket, you have some beads: when the beads are loose, you have a basket of confusion. It seems I can't make the beauty I wanted, so all right, I accept your help. We'll have a comradeship. I hold the thread while you, comrade, put on the beads, and little by little we'll make our necklace of commingled colors. I find beauty—you know where?—in a bill of indictment, the paragraphs all in a row, numbered and lettered, with no ambiguity, no aimless chatter. So tell me for the record, man: doesn't it seem to you that a person's life is like beads without a thread, all mixed up in the basket of our daily dayness?

I'm sententious? It's from dealing with lawyers and courts, notaries, police chiefs, prosecutors, judges. The dung beetle, you know, gets its shine from shit. I know every lawyer in every village around. The old boys like Salviano and Videira and Simão-Raposa still used that Latin hightalk, they knew their stuff, no prosecutor ever jagged them around. Juris doctors! But the kids that practice now, their talk is white sugar—it sweetens and melts to nothing. You never met Dr. Salviano? Then you don't know what a freezing fire is, or a tranquil tidal wave, or how you can be friends with a woman and in love with a man. You have to take it slow, real slow. . . . The lion has a tail: i.e., the earth is round. Theologies of Father Viêra. You don't accept unbiblical love and friendship? Your mind's got a long way to go, man. . . . Anyway, Dr. Salviano was once appointed to defend me, and he recited this Kimbundu saying: "If a white man strikes you, don't protest to another white man." That boggled the judge and he gave me six months—cushiest jail I ever did have. Pure cake. I was hoping to get condemned again with Dr. Salviano and his hightalk defending me!

A premeditated, unsuccessful attempt of homicide. That is, an unsuccessful homicide attempt. Which is to say, attempted premeditated homicide—that I truly and cold-bloodedly wanted to kill my girl, like a little lame bird whose neck gets twisted so the hunter can hang it from his belt—that's what the indictment charges me with. You'll meet her, man, she's coming by later on with some of her Bailundo specialties, and you're hereby invited to partake. Moamba stew from the Benguela-Catumbela lands. You never had any like it. She's a saint, the only religion I've got now. Which incriminates me in the testimonies. Listen, man, it's like this:

The way I am with people is different. I was born with good manners, I'm not a jealous sort, I learned that love tires, friendship refreshes. But if you never saw an ape lying in your bed, doing everything in the book with your woman, then you've no idea of the beast in your heart. An ape, a chimpanzee ape, that's what he was. His entire body a grimy white, his skin all buttery, without a bare spot showing, black hairs everywhere, on his back and chest, fuzz on his bottom. Pincers for legs, a bulging belly, and just one eye—the keen, quiet, perfectly still eye of a cat. But the worst thing was his smell. Believe me, man: I didn't back off on account of his monkey body squealing away on top my girl. It was his smell!—the stink of urine and sweat, the stench of his armpits worse than a coal-colored black man's. And my bed had embroidered sheets and a spread. I even had a little table with a lamp and three candles. If hell exists, then the smell down there is the same one he has—Mr. Ruas, a cornmeal merchant, a businessman from our shantytown, the neighbor that greets people by bowing down low. There was a moment that I even laughed—he couldn't get his feet back in his pants and he fell down, him and his bulging belly—but my

eyes were fixed on my girl backed up against the headboard, covered with drool from the ape, whom she im-
plored. Glistening girl, it's me that shines her body—I
know the lotions that make her skin tingle with a gentle
heat the whole night through. Her frightened teeth
murmuring in her funny Kimbundu, with that Bailundo accent I always did like. I ignored the white
chimp—he jumped out the window carrying his shirt
and leaving his shoes. Corroborative and material evidence for my defense, according to the lawyer the court
gave me, but I told him to forget it: I don't want my
trial to stink. Would you accept a freedom that de-
pended on a pair of shoes reeking with the toe scum of
a white-skinned cuckolder?

A woman is an unknown ocean, the depths. I'm
whole and solid—head, arms, legs, my sex. And she
agreed to a canker, to making jelly in a foul and ugly
pot, perverting the perfumes and lotions my hands had
left on her night-black body. I combed her hair, mas-
saged her scalp. I was only dozing, I never went to sleep
without taking a bath. Not complete? Me? You drawing
up an indictment, man? Impotent? I'm no giant, but my
equipment works fine—and, anyway, art's in the artist
himself, or do you think it's in his tool?

I vented my vengeance, a sweet sweet flame, a pa-
paya from Funda. All my words were tender, she trem-
bled in my hands. "My God, I'm all alone and they
want my life." She kept repeating, "I'm going to die,
I'm going to die," as if possessed by a spirit. I'm of
white birth, cross-fertilized. I had a normal childhood,
with a mother and a stepmother. Mulatto-without-a-god
is a lie, a calumny of those who envy our skin, our ways

with the ladies. I'm still suffering the suffering of that day—I'd like to drink that bitter sweetness again. I took a bath with her in the same tub, and I washed her and held her shivers in my arms. How red her eyes, like a turtledove's, when the white tears flowed! And we went to bed. A bed of colors. Sheets of freshness.

I lit the three candles of love and the censer containing the incense of falsehood. . . . I'm partial to virgins—a woman in my arms is Eve before the Fall. . . .

Unsuccessful homicide attempt—you're the water in my jug, man. Why are there so many ugly words in the law, so few in love? Do you see any relation between what I actually did, which they wouldn't let me finish, and all their complicated prattle? The law's a sham, man! . . . You know what I think? That in cases like this one all that counts is the film. They made me make the film, with my girl, the ape man, etc.—and the judge he had lunch, prosecutor he looked, lawyer he laughed. Then the law came along.

Words they lie.

My fate, it's like I said. She was the one that first foresaw it, which is why I give credit to any kind of spirit stuff—spooks and saints, voodoos and enchantments, mediums, charmers, priests and pastors. Because on that afternoon I was just barely eight years old—how is it I remember so well? I had three, yes, three loves that I'm going to lay out now so you'll get the whole picture. Because, as for all the others, I can't remember any of them lighting my heart the way those three did. Oil lamp in its biblical lamp stand, those days illuminate my life even now. In the egg you've already got the chick. Every color is the rain that bows.

It was after afternoon, me cuddled up in her lap, and she playing with my molasses-colored mulatto curls. If it had rained, she made it sunny—and I wanted to know: "Is it true about the meter?" And she laughed, with her tears well hidden, not sharing with me her sorrow, which I wanted—responsibilities. Because I only knew what I heard. My father was never one to use fool or foul language, and he was always saying, "The bastard! He cuts the electric meter off on his wife! . . ." And then my stepmother, with her nasty little bird face, she'd say, "Good for him! These modern girls all day long without lifting a finger. Serves her right!" And I'd see the doctor marking the meter numbers on a slip of paper. I wanted to kill him. Look at me, man: just giving you the record has got me killing him, making him kick, my hands softly squeezing. . . .

I'm an ingenerate malefactor, so said the judge. Hightalk of his I have yet to digest. You can explain it to me—later. Now I'm drinking my water in front of my stick-and-mud house, in our shantytown of the old days, and the doctor he already left for his office. My stepmother's looking for me to wash the dishes, my father went to work—he was a bread baker. Yes, he's still alive, but he doesn't exist, not anymore: he became a bakery industrialist. I'd sneak up next to her feet real quiet like, she'd be dozing on the veranda, protected by painted reed curtains: a colonial veranda like you never saw, man. And she'd open her eyes and let me get under her long dress, right up against her warm legs. She'd laugh. The damp and dry smell of those days won't ever leave my heart, man. I've been searching for it all my life since, in all the ladies I've had I look for it, but it's not there. It was the paradise of perfumes, in her and in no other. Then I'd lay my head in her lap and she'd play with my mulatto curls. But I didn't like her in the way she wanted—she wanted a baby doll, a kid to give candies to that I'd gobble down, to give a bath to when I got dirty, to console me in my disconsolation, my shame. And I wanted to avenge my tears over Sissy, I wanted to complete my friendship with him. Sissy was the only friend I had existed, and won't ever exist anymore. He was the third point of the star that's the first. And I'd ask her, "Is it true about the meter?," "Is it true about the radio?"—because her white-trash husband didn't want her listening to it when he wasn't there, begrudging cuckold that he was.

I asked my questions over and over, I wanted to see the tears she cried with me, at night, in my corner of the room, where I lived the most with her, deceiving Maristrela, who was mistress of that corner in the morning. She didn't cry, she laughed; she laughed and let me hold on to the soft breasts she had; she sighed. And I wanted to make her cry so that she'd be my responsibility, so that I'd get up the courage to do what I lived with her in my darkness: kill the doctor, make love to her.

Good God! My hatreds! Which I'm no good at keeping up—I forgive. Even her I've already forgiven: she slept with the chimp and is going to bring us some Moamba stew. . . . But him no—him I kill in absentia.

Listen, man: after lunch our shantytown was a pond without the sound of a pebble or frog. What ruled was the heat, hotter than what we get now, dead fire. Everyone slept. But I'd stay out on the walkway in front of my house and peer at the veranda with the reed curtains. And I'd see the doctor shut the blinds, after smiling at me through the window. And then came my torment: the shouts, the thumps, the commotion. Because I'd play hopscotch and hop as far as the fence. I liked to feel my little heart get hot, fill up with hatred, sweet venom inside my body; I laughed, probably even drooled, thinking of him, the doctor, squirming when I killed him. Because every single day he'd thrash the poor girl. He'd thrash her, I could hear it, but what I couldn't figure out is why she never cried, never screamed; it was only him I could hear, starting out real soft and getting louder until he shouted, always the same thing: "Electricity! Electricity! Electricity!" And my father he'd come to the door and pull me inside, sad as the flour in his kneading hands, and he'd mumble, "Bastard! Swine! The poor girl . . ." And my stepmother would gleam her old eyes in a gleam I didn't like, she'd laugh a scornful laugh, glumly gluing her eyes on my father. He and I we'd escape into the shade of the manioc tree.

And so every day my happiness was to fill my heart with hatred, sharpening needles for Maristrela, for our games with the birds. And I only felt sad if I thought of Sissy. When I was suffering for her I felt ashamed of Sissy, I didn't like him, I thought it was a sin. Now I know, and I already asked you your opinion: friends with a woman and in love with a man, etc., can it be? Don't tell your truth, man, without hearing my lies— they're twins. . . .

And so, comrade pal, if on that afternoon it was sunny, in me it rained. I took my hand off her breast, jumped up on the straw rug, and pulled her white hand,

and she thought I wanted to go to our other corner, the dark one—and we went. But not to take off my clothes and get a bath and her kisses. I pulled my matchbox out of my pocket, and she sat down with me on the painted reed mat, she thought it was a game, the cool maidenhairs and ferns, that shaggy smell of the daisies. I don't care for carnations—they smell too sweet. I don't like overkill, I'm moderate. "Does he beat you?" And she shook her head no, she smiled, motherly. "He does, he beats you, I hear it!" And she opened her black eyes, coals I ignited holding on to her big bosom. She grabbed me: "You hear it?" "I hear it and I don't like it!" "Do you spy on us?" And I saw her face turn white, bluish white in the shade of our corner. I swore I didn't. "He doesn't beat me"—and she smiled at me and I felt my hatred growing and it wasn't just the doctor made it grow. "But he shouts, he makes a racket on account of the 'lectricity." And she laughed, she laughed—she pulled me out of her arms, scooted against the wall, and choked from her laughing. "Smack me on the back, smack me on the back"—and she unfastened her dress.

Listen, man: I'm back in the corner again, my heart racing. Life isn't so: what make it get that way? Everybody with a fate all their own. . . .

The most holy trinity, Lord forgive me, is how I see those days back then. Reverend Father Viêra is who explained me how the three-pointed star is just one. There was the doctor's wife; and Maristrela, the girlfriend I didn't love; and Sissy, the only one who as far as really liking I really liked, with his curly hair and big black eyes. And I'll never be able to have it again—all of me in all of them. It's not the same thing anymore—

the Kwanza River is dirty everywhere but at its source, or am I lying, man?

Don't write that down. Half-truths of a half-breed. I don't look it but I am. Of black birth, cross-fertilized. Well, at least I'm not a Luanda pantywaist. Ah! You discovered, did you? So what's your guess? You're my gladness, man, when you surprise me. Yes, I'm from the Ambaca tribe, from Golungo Alto, a backwoodsman if you like, but not a backwoods bumpkin. Bumpkins come from Icolo, Bengo, and thereabouts. In their land there are rivers, but they've got no water; water comes from the lakes. . . .

The one who'd studied—the doctor—was the trashiest white of all. In our shantytown, you see, we had white-trash and whites-with-class, we had mulattoes-without-a-god, half-breeds, and even some Verdeans. The only black family was the Vendavals, all the rest of us were equals. So anyway, he built his house there, with the very first roof tiles to redden our shantytown, and with a colonial veranda that he enclosed with colored reed curtains, always shut, jealous of his privacy. And then she came. No one saw her with veil and bouquet. She'd already moved in—the wedding took place right in the orphanage, it wasn't until their sunnymoon that they came to live in the shantytown. It's always like this I see her: if it was raining she was sunlight. Black black tufts, smooth and slinky around her small round face. "Chinaware," said my father sententiously, seated on a stool by the door and I between his legs. "Fine chinaware, a girl with class," and he stroked his black mustache with his flour-white hands. Ditto her eyes, their color. And that mouth—she'd give me pecks on the cheek and I'd shift my face so as to catch them on my lips. It was the taste of her gajaja fruit, her spit, that I wanted. And she'd laugh like a water jug in the silence of a house.

A poet? Don't insult me, man. I'm a poetist, I read the Bible, I never let that book go—in my situation I'm still hoping to see the land of promission, the milk and honey of the bed of freedom with my Bailundo girl.

Whitey-white trash indeed, my stepmother was. We'd comment on the girl's tiny feet, her long dress, her proper way of walking, and my stepmother would snort: "A lot of airs! Orphan lasses make whores of all classes. . . ." Because she'd come from an orphanage— only now had she been uncaged. And in the shanty- town everyone wept over the heartwarming story of the older man that had saved her defenseless innocence. My father he stoked the fire. Today I think of him, with his coal-colored mustache and his leavened words, and I ac- cept that he liked the orphan girl. But his love wasn't like mine: his was pure as pastry flour. Whereas I wanted to avenge in her body, in her big bosom, the tears of my friendship with Sissy, and the uglitude of Maris- trela. I was already eight years old.

Is that what love's about, man—you tell me—re- venge over one thing or another?

Friendship in my book is like the January mist— welcome when it's dry, and welcome as we wait for the March rains. Love . . .

Let me also give you the record on Diodato, a white- with-class that got everyone riled. Just plain Diodato, he never even wanted to be called Mister. He was a Bolshevik, but meek and goodhearted. Even a little pathetic. Last name? All the less! He wouldn't consider it!

He spent the whole year wrapped up in his work. He spoke lousy Kimbundu and lived with a white girl. Never knew a white girl to shack up like that, only her, and my stepmother she was always badmouthing her, cutting her way down low: "A disgrace! All these different peoples, and the bad example comes from her. . . . How can we be superior? . . ." And once, when she got real worked up, I heard her use the cussword "slut." Anyway, on the first of May, Diodato would transform into something terrible! Early in the morning everybody'd wake to the sound of his hammer beating on the anvil for more than half an hour. Reveille! He'd also sing a song I can't remember anymore. . . . Hold on, man, I think it began, "Then, comrades, come rally . . . ," something like that.

Hey! You're my memory, man—sometimes you just plain amaze me. That's right: sounds like a dicole bird's whistle. How is it you know old-time things? Anyway, that's what he'd sing. He'd sing that song, and next thing we'd see him like we never did the whole rest of the year: blue suit, red tie, shiny shoes. Made of leather, patent leather that squeaked when he walked. And the kids they came running, his hands would pull candies and coins from his pockets, and he'd yell, "Proletarian brotherhood!" I'll never forget that word of his: proletarian. I got ten raps on my knuckles for writing what he said in a composition. My teacher was a white-trash bitch and let me have it. I swallowed my anger and my snot: the one she was coming down on was our friend Diodato—no Mister before his name, just plain Diodato to everybody, kids and grown-ups alike.

He'd disappear for the whole day. Only came back at night, drunk. Crazy drunk. And then he'd call his wife and give her a hiding like you've never seen. He smacked her with the same force and same rhythm he'd used in the morning when beating his hammer. Nobody tried to separate them: we were all too embarrassed, too afraid. We didn't want to ruin what we thought of him every day of the year but one. At night I hardly slept at all. But it wasn't out of pity for his wife, or because I was mad at Diodato—he was gentle, a Bolshevik, friendly. It's just that I was anxious for the sun to rise: Diodato's wife would come by, her face free of tears, smiling her resigned smile. And she and my father, who'd be wearing white clothes and flour and a red drowsiness in his eyes, would talk softly, the way I always heard them. She smiled a kind of happiness like I'd like to see in the faces of my ladies—it's what I'm always looking for. I'm obsessed with these good things tucked away in my memory. "Don't pay it any mind, neighbor, my man wouldn't hurt a flea. I know him inside and out, there's not a mean bone in him. But on this one day he always gets that way . . . since we been married." My white-trash stepmother, crass as they come, would cough when she said the word "marriage." But that didn't stop the smile: "Ever since we got married! Twenty-eight years ago. Like clockwork, I know beforehand. . . . But he really does like me, neighbor! If you only knew . . ." And I'd see my father smile like the saints on holy cards, and she'd twist her hands around in her apron and lower her eyes, a little embarrassed by the words she was saying.

I'm hearing—do you hear?—the chiming of bells in my ears: hammer and anvil in the early-morning dew, and the love of that smiling woman I wanted, before I die.

Take a good look, man, and tell what you see: is love the daily whatever, the newspaper? A come-and-go without an end?

Now have a laugh over this hightalk of theirs in court: Paragraph B, that somehow or other the some-thing or other, in virtue of the fact, it being the case that, wherefore, heretofore, henceforth, as it were . . . the doctor's report, wherein he swears on his honor that the sadist and heretic is yours truly. So can you give me a hand, wisdom of white hair on your still-boyish head?

Now you're at a crossroads! In hot water!

I'll supply the hound—now let's go into the woods.

Maristrela: never again did I see her, it's been al-most a century. She was the one I really loved. The points of the star—one, two, three. Ugly as sin she was, you'd never believe how such a runny-nosed, waxy-eyed child could turn out to be a fine-looking woman. They were all like her, all with snouts of hungry field mice. Seven siblings, rungs on a ladder, children of just one father and their mother, Dona Catita, a woman from the country. He was known as the Cape Verdean—we didn't know his name. Seated at the supper table, six boys and one girl before their chipped enamel plates, quiet and bug-eyed, just one dinky candle in the middle and a tall thin man hunched over, crying—you ever see anything like it, man? And a woman pouring hot water onto each plate with its spoonful of shantytown flour to try to fool hunger? They'd softly sing that mission stuff, hymns from the Kimbundu hymnal—doesn't it make you want to cry, man? I'd peek at them and run. Afterwards the kids would sing more mission, and the Cape Verdean would go out into the night—a bandit, it was said; he made trouble, it was said; he picked through the garbage cans downtown, it was said. Idle chatter . . . So I stopped feeling sorry for them, I mean the birds. I sharpened my knitting needles for her, Maristrela, pretending they were to pierce the eyes of the doctor, to make him go blind and die.

The sadist and heretic is me? Hold on, man: the facts by themselves don't tell the truth—you need the mind's thoughts. That's why I say Maristrela, my little Verdean, was the one I really loved. Undeniably ugly, the face of a field mouse, and yet she's the one who rules my mind to this day. She's in everything: she became a hooker when she was twelve.

The Cape Verdean, as I said, was a very Catholic man. Father of Maristrela and six other hungry field mice, a ladder of kids, misery. And he wouldn't take charity. He'd get fired from his jobs on the flimsiest grounds, but really it's because he was proud, reserved, self-assured. In our shantytown that kind of man had his friends and his enemies. I don't like people without enemies—they're beaten dogs, everyone feels sorry for them. My father praised him, my stepmother frowned. And I stole bread from the cupboard, along with some brown sugar, and took it to Maristrela. The Cape Verdean knew—he divided the half-pound loaf into seven pieces and almost smiled. I never did see the color of his teeth. But his long arms would grab onto me and sit me on his right knee and the youngest kid on his left, and he'd start talking that lingo of theirs, real mellow, that I like: "Our place is Cap' Verde. . . . Our land's a fair land—sluices full up with water, corn in the presses, and in Rebera, where we're from, we had a cow and cane liquor, lots of cane liquor, flowing to overflowing in the conduits of the sugar mill. . . . Yes, my little ones . . ." My father said he was from a hungry land and dreamed it into a paradise: fruit and milk and honey and the fluttering of birds. Or was it his language, those gentle words, that made everything he uttered seem beautiful? Words lie. . . . To this day I'm partial to Cape Verdean cooking, and how I love those sad mornas they sing.

I was saying: there weren't many Verdeans in our shantytown, it wasn't like now. There was Maristrela's father; Coino the stonemason; Fafa, an ex-boxer that slapped around his sassy daughters; Tuta, a woman of the night, a whore; Toi Barreto, an office clerk and a good man; and Vera-Cruz, a salesman, though I suspect he was actually from São Tomé. And old Pidrim, short fellow always dressed up in spotless white, he played the fiddle—but he needs a chapter all his own, man. First-rate confectioner, did miracles with flours and sugars, he was godfather to Maristrela, my ugly true love.

I'd get up early—early on his toes a little boy grows—and wander through the shantytowns along the shore, with my cages, traps, and birdlime. I'd peer into the bushes and my heart would thrill when a bluebreast or whydah bird trilled in their jails. Now tell me this, man: is it possible, at the same time, to be and not be? To like and not like, to feel pain and happiness, to have water with fire? In my love I hated Maristrela. The birds chirped, but I knew. I didn't want to take them, it tortured me when their singing halted and their warm feathers cooled, and I'd already be smiling with glee for making her happy, she'd even sing Creole songs before the sacrifice, and I liked seeing my sweetheart happy, but I was ashamed of hunting birds, creatures of the Lord of paradise.

We killed them like butchers, murderers, and drank their blood, she and I, heartless monsters.

You're right, man: I'm paying for my sins in jails, lockups, and prison camps.

But what about her? You can't render a verdict yet: the procession still hasn't reached the churchyard. . . .

I'd spend night after night sharpening my knitting needles. In the corner where I slept, on the matted floor—she there with me, my hand on her breast as I pierced the eyes of the doctor. With the smell of toasted bread under her dress. I live deep inside myself—things come, they go. Only she wouldn't go along—she dealt me a rejection that I still feel, pain of my happiness; she foretold my life's way, my wages of the cross; and I discovered that I loved Sissy more than her.

No, I don't mean Maristrela—alias Maris Stella, some dog-Latin I'll explain later—but my other girl, the second point of the three-pointed star, which is also the first. The orphan girl, from the institution. I opened my matchbox, she was already combing her hair after the smacks I'd given her to stop her choking. She didn't even look at me—she got up and left. But my lips had the acid taste of gajaja fruit, I'd thrown out two swollen rats, nailed in the night with my stepmother's poison, and I'd left my sharpened needles in the corner where I played with my Verdean sweetheart. I followed her all the way to their bedroom. She was in her slip, changing out of her dress. And she changed out of her slip—she was in her undershirt. And she changed out of her undershirt—she was down to her pretty embroidered black lingerie, a white lace bra, and her long panties with frilly frills, tied at her knees by yellow-rose straps. And she let me curl up in her smell, a toasty perfume I search for to this day with lotions and herbs, colognes and pomades, and all in vain! Does it only exist in my memory? And if I were to find it, would I then lose it forever? . . . She was entwined with me on her marriage bed, and I held on hard to my matchbox. I wanted to throw it out and just love my grown-up sweetheart—I was already eight years old. But she thought I was her son, and I wanted to pierce the eyes of the bastard doctor.

"Look!" She looked at my hand: "What is it?" I opened the matchbox. "Crumbs for the birds?" She had a pair of siskins in a wooden birdcage in the yard—Maristrela had already asked me to filch them for our ritual blood innocences. "No!" And I gave her a mean look, I wanted to look grown-up. "Then what's it for? For me?" My heart froze. If she took it by mistake or didn't wash her hands good, then would she end up being the swollen stiff rat while he, the bastard, went on living? "No, no, no!" "What is it? What are you afraid of?" I opened the box all the way. It had the crumbs my stepmother had treated with rat poison. She and she alone sprinkled them around, my job was just to toss the dead rats out back. She held me tight in her arms and I said, I whispered, "I want to marry you." I thought she'd get angry, mention the doctor, say I was crazy. She just smiled—I think she was even about to cry. "But I'm already married, don't you see?" She showed me her ring. I yanked it off and threw it away, into a dark corner. And she laughed. "I want to marry you." "And the doctor?"—she herself still addressed him as doctor. "I'll murderize, I'll kill him!" And I told her my plan for the poisoned bread crumbs, how she'd stir them into his breakfast. I even laughed: strychnine—a neat little word, like crushed glass.

Don't look at me like that, man: Paragraph B isn't only about being a sado-heretic—which I'm not, you'll see.

Didn't anyone ever give you a good whack on the ear, in the middle of your utterly still distraction? That's it—there's that hum that hangs on in your head, and stars wherever you look. Well, that's how it was—really! The whopping she gave me I spent I don't know how many weeks hiding from my father. I couldn't set my bottom on a stool, I couldn't sleep on my back. I bled at the nose and ears and mouth, and my nuts ached something awful, because she'd even tried to yank my dick off. Canine-lady, how I did like her. She's point one of the star, of all of it. And as she threw me off the colonial veranda and onto the street—she was wearing just her baby-making undies, which I'd ripped and bit into—she foretold my destiny: "You little murderer . . ."

Even today I carry around her smell all mine, love in its fullness and the words of blessing, all in her rejection of me. Her name was Tila and I still love her, I look for her everywhere. Fine chinaware, a girl with class—she gave me the body of Sissy.

So you tell me, man: love, what it it? Revenge?

Sissy—I don't remember his real name anymore. Or his face. It was his body I loved, we loved. Sissy for me, today, is this and just this: the only one that when I say "my friend" my heart beats faster. He's already passed on, under the ground, back to dust—I was there when he passed. I've seen my share of dead souls—kids and grown-ups and white-haired old folks—but the most beautiful of all was Sissy. When someone dies is when I enjoy partying—all night long, with a wake like you've never seen. I don't mind brushing against the phantom of Lady Death, the only thing I'm afraid of in the world is loneliness, that I do confess. With the dead I get along just fine. And the name he went by at home, his nickname, what he wrote on his schoolwork, and all the rest, I can't remember anymore. Just these words: my friend. And his big black eyes, always blinking, and his blond hair with the cruel curls, which we shaved clean off on his first day at school. But not one tear or cussword or cry. We teased him: "Are you a sissy?" No resistance, meek—he was the lamb, and we were the Jews. That's why I had to fight later on. And I fought every day. Every day of every week. Every day of every week of every month, a lot of them. Until finally Ginito and the others made peace with us: Sissy was mine, no one could insult him without insulting me. No one could lay a finger on him—he was my slingshot, my traps, my birds and green lizards.

Don't you know what it is to have someone that's yours, man, yours and yours only, someone who does whatever you want, no more mommy-daddy, I was the master, his God-and-Caesar? Then you've never been loved. He let us cut off his blond curls and didn't even budge to brush the hair off his shoulders. "Brutes!" he said. "Barbarians!" And I was the first one to call him a pansy, queerbait, fairy. He looked straight into my eyes for a long time. The others were waiting for my decision. Then he opened his hand that had always been closed and reached it toward me. "For you" was all he said. It was a shooter with a sun spinning inside it. Gorgeous glass marble, whose colors I only find after a rain in March when the sun comes out and the rainbow is a single whole with its starry cluster of colors. That day I went with him to his house, on the other end of our shantytown, a huge house tucked away in a garden, with his widowed mother and her maids and servants. Only child, spoiled rotten. I had to help him climb over the fence—he didn't know how.

He didn't know anything, which is what I most liked about him. Nothing of anything, nothing of nothing, when it came to using his hands. He was mine, I was his master—and I was his slave laborer, he my lord. I even unbuttoned him to pour out his waters. His only wisdom was this: the beauty of a flower in its own plant.

He couldn't handle a slingshot, wouldn't set a trap, didn't know how to dig a hole, or jump, or run, or climb trees, or fight, or tease, sing, whistle, play, steal—nothing in God's green world. Just think, man: he couldn't get a cork out of a bottle, it'd break and fall inside. You think it's funny? You'd cry the way I'm crying: he's the most useless beauty of my life. Friend gone to dust, dust and more dust.

But when he learned, then he was the soaring bird, the rest of us just clumsy ducks. Imagine: he couldn't sharpen a pencil—I was the one who did it for him at school. And I put the nibs on his pen and turned the pages of the green hardback—we always sat together at the same desk. Man, you'll never be able to see what I've seen, never know what I know—so how can you legally pass a sentence on our adulterous, incestuous love? And his handwriting—the colored flowers, the tails of his capital letters, whydah birds perched on the lines, the little loop on his O that seemed it was going to slide right off, Rs like the hoops we pushed along with sticks. And he drew birds, flowers—never houses, never people—clouds, the sun, and the animals. But the colors he came up with! You ever see a chicken the color of a reverend bishop's cape? Or a pitch-black flower? Or tree leaves striped and polka-dotted like a partridge?

With an avocado pit he drew the J on my white smock, on the pocket of my heart. And on the cover of my notebook, wetting his white white lips against the red of his felt pen, he drew my name with circumflex flowers: Juvêncio Plínio do Amaral.

Our loveship lasted not quite two years—death, life and resurrection, consecrated host. . . .

Juvêncio with a u, that's right. João Vêncio, too—and others . . . João Capitão, alias Francisco do Espírito Santo, alias . . . The honorable judge he just calls me Alias. To flee from the law, from responsibilities? Like hell! You believe that, man? I used to think judges and juris doctors were magnates, but they're about as smart as nails trying to swim, or toads that would fly. Ah! Man, you're my shade under the manioc tree—I'm refreshed by the breeze of your mind. You agree with me about the magnates? You're with me? Then let's go: Charlemagne and Oliver his knight.

I like changing my name. But what I really like is

changing my life. I can't take living for long in the same house, same road, same town. I'm forever changing my bedroom—rainy season and dry—and rearranging the furniture. My mustache comes and goes. Women, too— never did I love anyone again after my three-pointed morning star. My Bailundo girl she's a case apart. . . . And I change my hair color. None of which they understand in the proceedings. The toads! Each face with its own name, its own address, its own life—but I never make a move until I finish the job I'm on. I study what I'd like to be, what I want to do—I sow, I fertilize, I give birth to my life. Live life with nothing but my father's last name, birth certificate, identity card? I had a dog and changed his name once a month—he wagged his tail, happy as could be. Animals have feelings, you know. The only thing I'm afraid of, man, is solitude. My house is the house of one lady, always, whom I honor by living just for her and with her alone. I even had a government job, salaried clerk, for one year. Uniform and all. She liked that, she did—I mean the mulatto girl I ruined, she came from a good family. I tried to please—I'm the slave of my loves—but I finally had to leave her. She wanted too much bourgeois this and bourgeois that, and I can't fill gourmet bellies with the sweat of my brow. Yard work, shining shoes, selling papers, lottery tickets, waiting tables, traveling as a trucker's helper—that's what I do—manual labor that just buys your basic grub. No one gets rich with me, man. Larceny? I've never touched a grain of corn from another man's field. You can look at my record—an intermediary isn't a crook, I live by honest commissions, I rockefeller a bit. . . .

Well, man? You going to leave me in the woods?

You're quiet but you don't consent: I admire your silent arrogance. Life is so incomplete. If I could, I'd be a crusade; every day a different way; everywhere a different air. What I'd like is to be always somebody new.

Is man a domesticated animal?

You're astonished by my vocabulary, my patois? I already gave you the formula: my court trials plus the Bible. But the etc. is what proves the rule: Reverend Father Viêra, from the seminary. He's the one that opened my ears. He blew the wind of his Latinese on me and I forgot drawing and the numbers I liked. From then on all I wanted was amo-amas and gallo-bellicus. My getting expelled is a grief that still grieves me—I'm all for the Mass, but for saying it, not just hearing it. I'd still like to be a Reverend Father, lord of the Sabbath.

You think it's funny, man? Well, I'm glad. . . . Marrying fire and water in your justice hall. I have a hunch I'll get your acquittal for Sissy's and my love. . . . Anyway, my father it was that got me hooked: he gave me the dictionary opened and shut, I learned it by heart. Then, too, my shantytown, with its thousand colors of people, its thousand voices—I'm partial to Verdean lingo, all those neat words! And the rivers of my days, my ways: I was also a tour guide, you know, showing sailors the sights, clubs, hussies and sluts. I learned some English. *"Gee! the clean dirty smell of this sweet old she-rat . . . How much? Twenty dollars? Vêncio, tell this old crab I would rather fuck myself. . . ."* Ay-ay! My bad ways, parlances!

So where was I, man? Between Golungo and Cerca, lost in the Sala-Kabanga woods?

The basket's almost empty—you're an expert, man, in arranging colors. The bead necklace is looking fine, my Bailundo girl she'll feel my kitten spit on her paw, like as if she'd been licked. You be the guest of honor, comrade pal, for the southland specialties she's bringing. Stop twitching your tail like a whydah: "Whoever eats well thinks well"—pity I forgot the Latinese for that saying I read on the sly, in Reverend Father Viêra's cell. I respected his imprimatur. . . .

Religion? All of them! You ask the craziest questions, man! . . . The mulatto is a without-a-god? Like hell! I sang mission hymns with my sweetheart Maristrela and her brothers and mother in Sunday school. I drank holy water and wine from reverend fathers. I was an altar boy, in charge of the cruets. I let my wings grow—I marched in processions, straight and tall, with seraphim feathers, melting in the sun, intoning the Gloria and Agony-Day, crusade cross on my breast, knight of the Grail, defender of the faith. The lies, the lying lies they tell: calling me a heretical heathen!

They should have been there to see my eyes weeping at the feet of Our Virgin Lady, the wax from the torchlights of my soul streaming down my face, with the hellfire heat of the spirit I never did ever confess to my reverend-father friend Viêra. My sufferings of Saint Sebastian, nailed by blind arrows, or of Saint John de Brito, eaten up by cannibal pagans. I don't care for Saint Anthony of Quifangondo, he's too smily. A saint doesn't smile, man. In church did I never have serenity or peace there. I'd enter, wet my hand in the holy water, and right away feel the fire burning. My demons wanted to flee—all of me would twitch, each word of Latinese was a cold drop of hell, and the demons would gnash inside my heart, dogs howling at Father Viêra's Latin hightalk. I didn't miss out on his Masses. I was his apostle, his disciple. . . . What I like most in Catholic Mass is exactly that: the Latin hightalk chasing away the shrieking demons, a goad up their red bottoms. But Latin is words not meant to mean anything, just sound: organ music on the Lord's day.

What's that? You're the one who's telling me and I trust you, but I doubt it. Mass in the lingo of just anybody? Even in English, the language for picking up hookers in ports? Even in the German of the Naziistic monsters that killed the Jews that mocked the Lordje-sus? In Kimbundu, the language of miserable dogs? Go on, man! . . . You talk, and your water's my thirst. . . . But this is hard to take—I'm going to send for a book to find out the truth. Sorry—I can't believe that the holy sacrificial Mass can be said in just any old gibberish. Without Latinese, without vobiscums and hossanas?

Look, man: if we understand everything, then where does that leave God, our holy Heavenly Father?

If God exists? If you doubt, then he exists: that's the proof. Theologies of a reverend father whose name I forgot, all I remember is his local nickname, from the backwoods where he came with that beard, and he'd visit us every hundred years or so: Kamujinha, Father Kamujinha, who unlearned Portuguese and began to eat with his hand like a capuchin monkey. Maybe it was old age—his beard and his hair, white as white flour. He'd laugh like a kid and talk about tiny things: the life of bees is what he understood.

He'd go into trances, possessed by Vúnji, Kazola, or some other spirit in séances in the forest—his exile from the heavenly hosts. He died, without me getting a chance to see him, in the woods way north, where he'd gone to live. It was he who opened the doors for me of all the astral spirits, their story, incredible legends.

But what everyone talks about is that famous last séance, with a thousand pigs and all kind of chickens, swarms of gods, the ground swept clean, drums and rattles, the magical words battling the air. Persecuted spirits, flying in the astral sphere. And our Father Kamujinha, his beard shaking, waving, his white head wagging, coaxing the dead spirit. It came in a fury. Whoever saw such an old oldster hopping around like a young goat, marching as if to war, babbling phrases in some alien tongue, words garbled in his throat, his arm in a continual stiff salute as he twisted, twitched, and swaggered with a spirit? "Alleluia!" cried those who saw him. It was the spirit of a Germanophile führer, a Nazi, lost and wandering through the deserts, pursued by famished dogs—but he only told this at the end. Because first there was the battle. He wouldn't give in easily: to get hold of him, our father-of-the-gods Kamujinha had to put up a hard fight. "No! Not in an ape-man!" groaned the damned soul. "I'm no ape! In a black man, no!"—riding on the poxeclyptic beast, howling, refusing, no way he'd willingly enter the holy father whose face was covered over with cottony whiskers—the spirit thought the white man was black under that beard! Father Kamujinha fell to the ground and subdued the beast, who converted, repenting his Naziistic crimes. Kamujinha they had to carry in a hammock through woods and more woods, to an outpost with a clinic. The bishop exonerated him and he died, so it's told, like a little bird, chirping psalms.

He's in Our Lord's heaven, a beekeeper: his business is honey for the baby angels, wax for the candles, and his beard will never again get cut. But this is a secret, man—divined by Petelu dia Kimbungu, renowned father-of-the-gods.

Every religion is true, I believe in all of them—a lesson from Kamujinha that I accept. I've seen a Muscleman squatting on the deck, turned to the holy Mega, chanting his blah-blah-allah. And a three-legged table that answers back answers, and a fortuneteller at a fair making her movie in a crystal ball. Because I'm not a party man. My celebrations are the sorrows of others— funerals. To happen on a good funeral, with lots of tears, the weeping of old ladies—young girls now don't know how to honor the dead with their tears, which is a scandal. Condolences, obituaries, the sifted virtues of the departed, badness belonging only to life. The night rolls along, no sun to spoil things, a little light is a lot—and there are the fabulous tales of nights and more nights, the barking hyenas, the telling of tough riddles to keep the brain from falling asleep. No one announces his verdict, life or death or happiness, without a proverb to escort it. A good proverb is worth a treatise, man! "The death of someone else's child is the time for spinning cotton." . . . And then the wake. To celebrate the fortune of the departed soul—a wake with fireworks, food and drink, and hurdy-gurdy music, eating until you burst, and what's left goes to the sea, the man dies, his fame lives on . . . hooray!

I like to amend, to correct life.

I lit the three candles of love and arranged them on the nightstand. I burned the cannabis incense in the thurible, to fumigate. And she wanted to smile her palm-oil charm, but the chimpanzee was still there, in the bed. She kept repeating incantations in her Umbundu dialect: "Vayongola o mwenhu wange!"—"They want my life!" The room filled up with the perfume of the burned leaves, a holy-jesus of scents and burning candles, like as if it were church. In the Mass of love, the candles on top the altar, the saint below. But first I tore away the sheets and bedspread and threw them all out the window. Clean linens—a sheet with a heart embroidered next to the headboard, a fresh violet bedspread, I grabbed my southland lady and laid her on the bed, I celebrated. Room shut tight—the incense couldn't escape. I opened my ointments, the one for hair, with European roses. And on her Jamaican chocolate body I used a lotion I got from Gino, a Genoese sailor, amico mio, unguento d'amore, cool menthol that pricked the blood. For myself I stuck to cologne, fidelity. What I felt like was crying. She's so tiny, round like an O, like a little doe curled up on the bedspread, I was already weeping her departure. But first I did my malefactions, I roughed her, I roughed her real bad. . . . Till I no longer recognized my girl—she seemed, yes, like the railroad: train is what moves, she was just the tracks. I yelled: "Think you can cheat on me? Think you can cuckold me?" She just prayed like the Madonna: "Vayongola o mwenhu wange. . . ." Slaps on slaps, pinches. She slid out from under my body, I derailed. I saw the chimp shrieking on top my Bailundo girl and she going right along in the hither-thither of an alligator catching a scent. She shouted but I held her down to the bed and squeezed her neck. Man, look here: the hands of a deep love. I always like to see a woman close her eyes when she's with me. And she slowly closed them, I liked how she snuffed out the light of her soul, I traveled with her through the sandy shantytowns toward heaven, our souls united. I never did know such peace. When I reached the police station my wandering soul was still asleep, still not back from its journey, lost among those shantytowns I saw with my dying Bailundo girl. They revived her in the hospital. The chimpanzee ape took the thurible, candles, ointments—my whole village of love things—to the station. In the proceedings they're evidence. Paragraph B—sadist, heretic, and you name it. Toads! Blockheads! I'm an educated man: is a beautiful woman a mere hole in the ground for a game of marbles? Every woman is an Our-Lady. I'm delicate, I don't believe in evolutionism. Man descended from the apes? Like hell! I'm from divinal origin—Mr. Ruas, cornmeal merchant, isn't a person.

Here I'll make a parenthesis. You're open-minded, but still I hesitate. The honorable judge, the prosecutor, and the other bossmen of the law they only see the straight line, they're blind to the narrow door. As far as the police, I'm not surprised—they're res publica. But that I was jealous of the cuckolder ape man, that I was furious he'd moved in on me, that I was seething with vengeful rage—imagine! How can someone who doesn't know me know? A lady belongs to everyone, only to you if she's the one that wants it that way. I don't like to be god over anyone. But beauty is mine, that's my honor—and the white chimpanzee shat on it. I had to clean the sheets of his simian coitus—the world's beauty is my aquarium.

This is between you and me, man. One day I ran across an ant with a tricolored body: red, black, and yellow. In a line of black ants, an ugly deviation. I kept it and fed it for almost a month. I cried over its death in the clutches of a hairy spider.

Water and fire, friend of women and lover of a man? The prettiest woman's name I ever heard belonged to the sluttiest slut of our shantytown: Florinha. They set fire to her hut, tied and thrashed her, and sent her off to the prison at Tiger Bay. And that name is my star's center: Florinha. How I miss her, man, how I do miss her!

Now I think you're ready, man, to be my judge. I told you about the birds. I'd catch them around ponds with a birdcall and seed, and the trap was the lie I told them. I betrayed them. Even today, when I see a bird in a cage I free it, I steal it so I can free it—because I have a guilty conscience. People should have pure, distilled hearts, so that birds would have nothing to fear. They would see, understand, and come land on our fingers, careless warblers. If they sense wickedness and flee, imagine if they sensed goodness! . . . Yes, my heart was divided, not into the auriculars and the ventriloquists, but on the one side my love with Maristrela, living together as man and wife in our nook of innocences and dolls, and on the other side the chirping beauty of my singing birds, God's creatures that He never banished from paradise. Yes, I hunted, lured, and trapped. I filled up the wooden cages. I even mixed the belligerent birds in with the lazy ones that are the prettiest: gungos with whydahs, red-beaked sparrows with hummingbirds and kingfishers. Sometimes on my way home I'd set a few loose—I suddenly couldn't stand it. But my heart would mutter, "The eyes of Maristrela!" And I'd see them shining their Verdean shine as she stuck in the knitting needles I'd sharpened. That was our game: blind the poor creatures to make them sing better. Honest, man, I swear it's true! When blinded, the siskin and the Kwanza canary sing like crazy. What's that? Do I think pain purifies beauty? You and your questions, man! Let my birds alone—I don't want weeds to grow back in my remorsified heart.

She's the one that poked their eyes out. How she did shine, and the eyes, and the needles, in our little nook. She sang Creole lullabies while rocking her dolls, and I was the hangman of the Queen of Kashmir—in the heart of every singer there's a Cupid's arrow, a knitting needle.

At night she and her field-mice brothers, the whole lot of them, with their father, the Cape Verdean, and their country-bred mother, Dona Catita, they'd all stuff their tummies with bird-and-rice stew. And then one day Maristrela came down with hummingbird disease: you get it from eating the tiny bird, and sores break out on your head. Her scalp started scaling, all her hair fell out, her face got scurfy. We scrubbed her with hot palm oil mixed with herbs that Dona Catita had to go to Dande to get. Unsightliest sight you can imagine, like a huge and hairless she-rat. Until her twelfth birthday. Ugly, ugly, ugly, and the one I loved the most. And then her breasts sprouted and her periods began. She went to the white man Katonho's place and became a whore. Her family started to eat right; her brothers even went to school. A blessing. She changed: from the trash heap that was her childhood body emerged a lovely lady, a pubescent beauty. Her eyes still with their shine from when she stuck in the needles, her face now full and round, a star, beautiful, hair like a peacock's, done up with lotion. And her body was like a pillow of eczema— all those people that slept with her would get the itches, taking pain and pleasure as they scratched away. They told me all this: I never had enough courage to say so much as good day after she went to the white-with-class Katonho's place. I'm shy by nature—in our little nook all I wanted was two things: the cobra shine of her eyes as she stuck in the bifid needles, and the birds' warm blood to drink. We'd lie down, sleeping man-and-wifely, the Queen of Kashmir and the Grand Visor, but I never so much as lifted the tatters of her skirts. In my book she's pure purity.

Love: a fish stew without any fish, just morsels? The fish isn't much, we're never satisfied. That's why I loved the toasted smell of the legs of Tila the orphan girl. I wanted to marry her, in the doctor's bed—I was eight years old. And I took the white body of my friend Sissy into my arms, next to a faraway pond, on the day I saw my first chimpanzee ape: trained in the law, hysterical.

I learned my philosophy early on: it's possible to vary, to multiply without cheating. To love just one woman alone is a very incomplete thing.

Me and Sissy, me and my friend, our love, our friendship, our loveship ours alone—homoerotic perversion is what the judge would say if he knew. But I could never tell it: my purity would be their dung. With you I'm in the woods, man, we use the same hound, we're comrade pals. You have a child's heart, your flour-colored hairs came early, they're the fingerprint proof. . . .

After the lunchtime drowsiness and the pampering I got from my girl the doctor's wife, I'd take off. I'd whistle my whistles and he'd come running, slave of my know-how but master over me with his big eyes. He even wore shoes and a white T-shirt. We'd fly away laughing, behind the butterflies and grasshoppers, all the way to the ocean. He's the one who taught me to say the word like I say it—a seashell echoing in your ears, man. Ocean! And we'd hide his clothes among the rocks of the lighthouse, and I'd dive in with my all-occasion shorts, so grimy with oil they were waterproof. Sissy was a drifting grouper in a blue sea with a yellow floor— naked his body was all one white. Head to toe, just one color. He'd come out of the water, shake his long blond hair, and lay down at my side. Two eggs incubating in the hot sand, joking around. I didn't tell him about my grown-up girlfriend, the bastard doctor's wife, or about Maristrela, but it was with my old craving for ugliness that I'd cover his whole body with sand to make it dirty. Because his skin was satin, without a single spot or moth. After I dirtied him, I'd fetch cool water in my cupped hands, wet him, give him a bath, wash him. And then vice versa. He'd laugh at my dark body: "Don't you use soap when you wash?" "It's God that made me this way!" And he smiled, his blond strands all wet. "You're a liar: God only made white people! You need soap." One day he brought lavender soap, which now I like so much that when I see it I take it. And my stepmother swiped it from me, she washed her stinky hide with my angel's delicacies. "Ugly!" he said, grabbing my dick. An innocent. I was the one who felt ashamed and made a fuss. He never once got angry. We'd sit down—two nudes and the ocean. Next to my flattish face, his elegant nose breathing in and out. "Say it: ocean!" And I'd say my closed vowel sounds. "No! Ocean!" His pink mouth, the waves' foam in his teeth. He kept trying, he'd pull my lips into a big O: "Ocean!" Until he found the yellow seashell. He kneeled before my darkish body, resting the shell against my right ear. And I heard his mouth, his word in my ear, in my chest, in my heart. I said, "Ocean!" And he laughed. He laughed and said, "Ocean!" And I kept yelling, "Ocean! Ocean!" He stood up, shell in hand and me with him, arm in arm: "Ocean! Ocean! Ocean!" We walked until the water burbled in our mouths, hand in hand, into the ocean-sea.

With him it was pure friendship, it was rainwater, and more.

It was the rain joined our bodies behind the wall of friendship. Swimming, we discovered anemones on the sea floor, and we saw the grouper's brilliance—scaly and silent—right before our eyes, under the water. We stared at the sun, to see the world's shadows. I swear, man: the world belonged to us, we were always skipping school, the whole world to us, the lords of peace and war—but our hearts weren't full. Friendship is a scanty meal for children's hearts. Is friendship only for grown-ups—is it a walled prison with Christian decency standing guard?

The roaring of thunder and flashing of lightning

over the surging sea—and we, two wet chicks in the dark of a fisherman's hut. We hung our clothes to dry in the warmth of the coconut leaves. And we dried our bodies with our burning, sunburned blood. We stood face to face, angry we weren't as man and wife—our little chick members poking out and hitting, each one wanting to hide in the other. My rage flared, I cried, I thought of Maristrela lying down with me in the birds' feathers, just to be together, because I never wanted to do anything naughty with her; and the orphan girl Tila, whom I wanted to marry, and she treated me like as if I was the son of the womb of her pain. Revenge—is that what male love is?

My friend, Sissy—the only one that when I say friend, my heart starts to wander. With him, yes, we could have gone ahead in the innocence of paradise, but God didn't want it—out little dicks hit each other, enemies.

God or maybe the demon devil, the horned Bells-a-bub?

God is whatever we still haven't lived. What we're living is of man, it's us. And what's been lived is of the devil, to frighten others.

Don't write that down, man. You embarrass me: idle talk of a half-breed and you think it's gold? It's just pinchbeck. . . . I want to get to what I promised to tell; there's not much thread left, the beads are multiplying in the bottom of the basket, my Bailundo girl is going to wear the colors you weave. Shall I be frankly frank? You've got an eye like a painter of pictures. My Sissy he colored at random, without rhyme or reason, and on the page of his notebook his sun was always shining. Whereas ours was just a tiny candle, a snuffed

stump, a bitty wick. . . . But the teacher didn't like
Sissy—the blind-souled bitch. . . .

What I promised, all right: the chapter on Mr.
Pidrim, the other Verdean whose parlance I still haven't
told. First of all, summarizing: my shantytown's white
folk included white-trash like the sterical doctor; the
merchant Zuba, a mean son-of-a-bitch that wouldn't let
anybody buy on credit; the policeman Officer Ventura,
more respectable, but his phonograph played a broken
record—billy club, club, club . . . ; and the rest that
don't matter. Then there were the whites-with-class: Mr.
Katonho, who never put water in the wine or cheated
on the produce scale, who made Maristrela into a whore
and did away with her family's hunger; my own father,
modesty aside; a few others. Blacks there were none,
except for the Vendavals at the very top of the shantytown: a huge house with lots of land, and a name that
mattered. They coupled up within the family, real snobs.
Kept to themselves—landowners and office workers that
didn't say so much as hello. The kids from that house
never played with us, as we were too low-class: white-
trash, Verdeans, and mixed-breeds. On Independence
Day they ate at the Palace banquet. . . . All the rest of
the people in my shantytown—I never heard different—addressed them each one by their proper name,
preceded by sir or madam or doctor or lady and so on
down the line. Niggers, baboons, black scum—these
names I only learned later, from Sissy. I already told
you about the Verdeans from Cape Verde—Coino and
the rest. Did I mention two-dollars-a-night Tuta? Then
the only one left is Mr. Pidrim, stout and dressed in
ducks—a singer of mornas and a confectioner by trade.

He's the one who taught me not to like women on

sale. To luxuriate in love. I never went in for meretriciousness. Not my style. With me a rank whore turns into a lady. I never pay, I don't know how to use money to exploit. Love is in the pleasure—giving and receiving. I never leave a woman with her eyes open.

So, anyway, this Mr. Pedro—Pidrim in the way he talked—was from Brava Island. He told stories of whaling ships, of a grandfather whose name and sword were in a museum in America. A Verdean that was fat and bowlegged—"stout," he translated, his gold buck teeth laughing, a man of means. He'd risen up from nothing, a self-made man: started as a baker's helper, my father gave him a hand—he grabbed his foot and became a kneader. A needy kneader—he held my old man's hand tight, climbing past him on the malumbu tree: he became a dough shaper. My father was never one to get envious of other living souls, he always knew where his own place was, and it beats me how he got to be a gentleman industrial exploiter—maybe my nasty white-trash stepmother cast a spell on him. But Mr. Pidrim wasn't a hen to lay eggs in a strange yard—he took wing. With Mr. Coino he built an oven, he himself. Sweet sweets, hands of honey, doughs like dreams—flour in his blackish hands was dry fallen dew that melts in your mouth. But I'm getting off track. . . .

He was always dressed in white, to a T; later on it was an English duck-cloth jacket. He was even called in at the governor's Palace. He was a somebody—only thing missing was to take a wife, people said. That's when I met him.

Now, consider, man: whoever rises up, his shadow's a shelter for a lot of folk, but it darkens. . . . The ungrateful want the coolness of the lazy shadow and the shining of the sun at the same time. . . . So, being envious, they rumored around that he was a pansy.

He always paid his bills; his gold smile greeted white-trash, mulatto hybrids, and coal-colored blacks without any conceited discriminations. Everyone liked and respected him. We were careful not to get his jacket grimy—only after he took it off did we hang all over him to get the pastries he made from leftover dough, and never ever did he let us down. He'd make a whole ovenful just for us. He didn't lift up single girls' skirts, and he knew the right words to show respect for married women. He'd lend his money without bankers' interest—he lived amid swindling parasites and smiled. He never went to Zuba's store, he didn't use swearwords. He took a daily bath—he it was hauled the water. Decked out in white, with cologne. He composed and played mornas on the fiddle, weeping with feeling. He was godfather to my Verdean sweetheart, Maristrela— Maris Stella Lopes Barbosa, the dog-Latin name he pronounced with his gold smile, his floured hands. . . . Where does the heart of darkness find an arrow for an angel like that?

The rumor, the dirt: that he fooled around with little boys, that's what his pastries were about! Sweets? . . . Sweet nothings!

Vicious lie of scoundrels. In fact he was a regularized customer of Tuta—and it was out of love. "Remember, boys, that a lost woman endures a lot of suffering. We should comfort, not blame. . . ." He never gave her a single dollar, not even a copper coin. "A woman is sacred, she's not to be bought. . . ." He'd give her a basket of sweets, his very sweetest, creams and honeys. But not on the days he did hanky-panky with her, with Tuta, the night woman. "Never pay back a favor. A golden rule!" Three or four days later he'd send her the basket, one of us would take it, and Tuta would eat everything right on the spot, all by herself, a dog with her bone. Not even a crumb, we just watched her gorge, nothing. She'd hand us back the basket with its fine lace doily and burp behind us: "He's a cheap-skate!" But who could have made a more groundless affirmation? When an old woman dies and next day the panther defecates white hairs . . . He made love with Tuta, and she's the one who unleashed the poison rumor: that he was a pansy, a queer.

Slander is a lizard's tail—cut, it still lives. . . . It grows back! The grown-ups forbade us to accept his sweets or go to his house. They tried to get us to make fun of him with songs and names. They poured water outside their doors just as he was passing by, spattering shantytown mud on his English ducks. Stones would whiz over his shack's zinc roof. Days and weeks and months of vile pranks. Until finally, on Christmas Day, he went to the sunrise Mass and then lay down in his bed—he departed from the valley of poison tears, he suicided himself. He cut his wrist, letting all the blood he had flow into the enamel chamber pot he'd placed next to the bed so as not to dirty the floor.

"He bled himself, the impotent chicken," was my stepmother's requiem. And the government appropriated his shack, he was never mentioned again, amen.

Lies, man, are like this: the devil's flour with angelic whiteness in our hands.

Prostitutes, tutes, tutas . . .

Florinha is forever crossing my mind—how different she was from Tuta the Verdean.

In the old days the shantytown was full of loose women. Nowadays they're more discreet, more dispersed, but back then they were like the flying ants that come out when it rains. Of every kind imaginable, and without any shame. There were ordinary old whores, meretricious mistresses, corpulent courtesans, adventuress actresses, concubines, kept women, and paramours. In the local lingo: the quiuaias, who went out on the prowl, wild cats grinding their teeth; the quitatas, who'd stand in the doorways, shaking their hips and wagging their fannies, whistling at the wastrels that wandered by; the munhungueiras, mongrel bitches that sniffed out their mates and did it right in the grass. Such a beautiful name on such an ugly face. Her real name was Florinda, Christian baptized. She was Florinha for us, Dutcha for the Cape Verdeans, and Kangüeta—which meant "poor white"—for the landowners, even though she was three-quarters black, tall, with large gaps between her teeth and a broomstick for a body. She was vain, and dressed kind of kooky. Barefoot inside her shack, with just a cloth wrapped round her bottom. But when she went out, we didn't know whether to laugh or cry: perched on high heels and wearing a gangly silk dress, the hem of her slip smiling. She even carried a Chinese parasol, rain or shine, that was missing the ribs—she always wanted to look like fireworks. An honest-to-God clown! How is it that we kept from laughing, respecting her daffiness better than the grown-ups did? We'd seen the terrible. We'd witnessed death's cruel coitus with

Ninito—no one else knew, just us. But I don't have it in me to tell you, let's let the record rest awhile—the beads are heavy, the thread is stretching, if it breaks I won't be able to see my southland lady flash her contented firefly eyes. . . .

But listen: to end the pain of a cruel death, is it permissible to commit murder, infanticide?

I've talked too much about death, suicide, homicide, and other cides; you're going to think I'm the undertaker, who measures the coffins. The thing is, I was born feet first, too much of a philosopher—even in happiness I lose my bearings.

Love is a star
We all pursue
With a lit candle
In a dark room. . . .

Surprised?! Stunned?! I sang in my own reco-reco band long before all these amateurs that shriek over the radio, cheap mercenaries. I was even the maestro master of Liceu, the singer. This samba was my big hit. There was an article about it in one of the city papers—a man went around swiping our tunes, and not a nicked nickel did we get paid by the congenital son-of-a-bitch. He wrote that it was an expression of the ero-philosophical soul, but the asshole didn't put down my name—and in those days he could have, I still didn't have much of a police record. They say it was written by Capopa, by Mirumba or Amado. Like hell! I know the genesis, exodus, and whole Bible of this samba. Say what?! By

Amado, a Kimbundu composer? A samba with this class, floating up in the heights, without his corniness?

> And when we meet,
> Out goes the candle
> We no longer need!

Ah, man, my feasts, my revelries!

Paragraphs A, B, and C, the adverbs of my accusation. You've got to laugh, man—here we are in the twentieth century, any day now our eyes will see the hand of man on the moon's face, and those lackeys of the law typed "enslavement, slavery, slavitude"! Every dot and tittle! "Furthermore, the concubinage effected by methods contrary to Christian civilization and aggravated by the misrepresentation of the defendant's inured practice of forming sexual liaisons outside legal matrimony, is indicative of a character that . . ."—so on and etc., I learned all their hightalk by heart.

What bunk! My Bailundo lady, object of my devotion, is the enslaved one? Sure, man, you'll see the marks of the shackles on her legs, her skinny wrists, the handcuffs she uses, the hunger she endures. . . . Never was I less free than with this savage slave.

She came from down south, an old pal of mine brought her north. He's a bigamous catechist who had the bad luck to be caught by the holy-mission fathers. Lived with a wife and his parcel of land in the peace of the Holy Spirit. And biked back and forth to court my Bailundo girl. He defiled her. He claims she'd already lost her virginity, he tries to pin the blame on the priest, but the creature knew so little that I don't believe it.

She was minus zero in love—I taught her all she knows. A Bailundo raised in holy Masses, she went all the way through grade school, in the vernacular, because in the southern missions they study in their own Kimbundu. I liked her altarly air, a saint sitting in the dance-hall chair. I noticed right away how she stayed clear of tempting devils, brute beasts, men with no scruples. The way she danced was so moral! Without any shimmy or shammy. I saw the raw material, the original word for me to breathe on and make flesh. "What's your name, sweet thing?" Her firefly eyes looked down, all embarrassed. "Don't you speak our Kimbundu?"—I'm stubbornly gentle. I saw the waterfall of a giggle on the corners of her lips. "Are you just modest, or afraid on account of your man?" The shine of her astonished eyes shot up. "I don't have a man. . . ." I never laugh at a woman's lies. I respect sentiments. "I beg your pardon!" I said, bowing my head. But a moment later: "What about him?" I pointed with my eyes. "That's my godfather. . . . " I knew I could smile then, her voice gave me the go-ahead. I saw her skin change shade, she was blushing—she was already within the territorial waters, the rights were mine.

He came right over, it was the three of us there: him looking at me and her with his cynical smile, the kidnapping catechist cad. "Caught you!" he cynicized. She a shy doe, eyes on the ground, hands twisting her scarf, a forest-green chiffon. The Don John—me—confident of my coastal rights. I was taking in the whole scene—the dance out in the yard, the reco-reco smiles, the shuffling feet, the voice of the singer, and us in the refreshment area, where beers were weeping their ice-cold tears. I love the theater, man. I never once went, no kidding. And how do you know you wouldn't like to die, man? Got you! Theological tricks of my Father Professor Viêra.

So a little while later I was under the manioc tree, relishing my corn beer, and he grabbed my elbow. He the sober one; me, soused. "She knows how to cook first-class, for a priest, and she has hands like an elf for sewing. You can teach her the rest, she's inexperienced. Grade-school graduate. Seventeen years old." He spat and looked me straight in the eyes: "Seventy-five dollars and a sewing machine!" I played the tycoon—I gave him my last hundred. "I'll get the machine to you on the weekend," I disdained.

I left the crummy dance with my arm around my Bailundo girl—the stars in the sky had all snuffed out, and the crowd clapped their hands at the doors, congratulating me.

Theater, man? It's paradise after the Last Judgment, my father would say of all that was beautiful and hard to obtain.

Enslavement? I was the one who was the slave of my loves—the three-pointed star with its center, Florinha, who wasn't even mine. Maristrela and Sissy, my old friend; and the orphan girl Tila, the doctor's wife, her toasted perfume under that velvet sky, in the warmth of her legs. I've even studied sorcery with plants to locate her: all in vain! I still look for her, I'll catch up with her eventually, even if I have to go to the Devil's paradise. I can't die without smelling once again her toasty smell and feeling her thresh-hand thrashing away at my illicit love.

I roamed around on my own. I rained pebbles on the zinc roofs, broke windowpanes, skipped school. As for Sissy, I stopped whistling across his fence, I abandoned him—my heart was too little for hatred. All I did was pierce the eyes of every living thing I hunted. I'd catch a green lizard, tie it to a totem pole, heap matchsticks all around, dance the dance of the Indians—Hunga! Hunga!—poke out the light of its eyes, and set it on fire. Once I seized the mother hen of seven yellow chicks and pierced her beady, irate eyes—she couldn't believe that the day of official darkness had come, end of the light of her life. I even laughed afterward, the hen blind and discombobulated, the little ones peeping on all sides and she unable to locate them. I couldn't sit still, I'd stare at her window after lunch, she no longer came to show her smile, the bastard dastard kept it closed. I'd follow behind women who were far from their homes to snoop on them doing their necessities in the bushes. I smelled all kinds of ureas of women peeing under the tambarino trees at twilight. In my sleep I sharpened knitting needles, and in my dreams I slobbered the laughs of a madman. Until finally it happened. Four o'clock, one Saturday afternoon. Silence—she appeared once again and smiled in the window. And the dastard bastard didn't come shut it—she filled up the whole window, a star. I had to cry, my hatred was too much, it ran out the veins of my heart. I leaned against the fence, heaving with tears. I snuck on in and went around the yard. The door was open like I knew it could never be again, for the doctor had the soul of a prison guard. I smiled at the siskins in the cage; they stopped singing, startled, afraid of my eye-plucking boy's face. I stole along like a thief. The living room: panic, I nearly shout. Cuckoo, just the wall clock. Four trumpets. Luckily I didn't even breathe a swearword. My heart's lazy beating speeded up—I waited. I was going to hide, let the nasty doctor leave, go away, so I could set up camp on my oasis, in the cool shadow of my two aphrodisiac palm trees, in the coffee-roasted perfume of all her flowers. I'd crossed the desert—now I wanted my harem of a thousand smells.

"Electricity!" I heard a voice murmur. Then louder: "Electricity! Electricity!" And the sound grated and got louder, along with the aching moans of someone being beaten and softly pleading pardon. And "Electricity! Electricity! Electricity!" The dirty son-of-a-bitch doctor was spanking my girl, as usual. I pushed against the door. Locked. And the spanks—from a swung board— grew louder in my ears. I remembered to peek through the keyhole.

It's like I said, man: if you've never seen a chimpanzee ape on top your woman, then you've no idea of the criminal that lives inside you.

He was the first rangotang ape to defile my loves. I peeked, I saw: rocking, panting, yes, he was the one shouting, "Electricity! Electricity! Electricity!"—in ecstasy, the scoundrel lying in the shade of my aphrodisiac palm trees, thurible of my perfumes. And she had smiled at me, inviting, seductive. She'd made me cross the desert and was now fornicating with the ape. She moaned. "Slut! Slut! Slut!"—my tears kept me from seeing where I was going, I bumped into a chair, I broke a clay pitcher in the corner of the veranda. Ah! I stamped up and down on the cage until all that remained was a pile of sticks and feathers and the blood of the happy pair of whistling siskins, holocausted by me, under my red feet. I yanked all the flowers out of all the pots, I tipped over the jug of fresh water, and I left—I was the whirlwind of the devil, somersaulting in vengeance, beast number seven, with seven heads.

I scrammed.

And he came. Whenever I whistled across his fence he came, a true-blue friend. He came, he came laughing, and I grabbed his hand and helped him over. His blond curls, those blinking eyes, big and black. His white cambric T-shirt, beige corduroy shorts, shoes with wide buckles—no socks. He noticed my red feet, which I rubbed against each other. "Blood?" I looked down. "Let's beat it," I ordered. He was with me, hand in hand. We ran on our way, we ran in May: through shantytown sands we ran ourselves ragged, through red sands, yellow sands, short grass, flowering cashews, bees, long grass, flowering mangos, the footpath—the pond, croaking tortoises, frogs like from fables. All was golden with the sun's honey pouring down. The blackish water, deep and still. The birds fluttering, flying, frightened at our intrusion on the beginning of their night. A thousand warbles, goldfinches. We took off our clothes, we swam. We dirtied our bodies, we washed them. And we sat down in our nakedness, watching the water, waiting for our mermaid. And she came: she was the night, just the start of it, with its cool rustle. Then he took my hand, squeezed it: "Juju, you're my friend, forever and ever?" I gave my word. "And we'll never separate, never ever?" I nodded my head, I wanted to cry. And I did cry, we hugged, I howled with weeping, hurting worse than when Tila slugged me in the corner of the room. And the moon loomed large above the muxixe tree, blue it loomed, we could see it rising in the sky, its weary face smiling. The birds cooed. "Let's go!" He grabbed my hand. But I felt I couldn't go back home until I got what I wanted, until I whistled for him to come under the tree. I wanted to be all, all to him, my friend. I hugged him, held him, pressed against his chest, we stretched out on the ground, in the grass, on the edge of the blue water, hearing the music of tree frogs, and he was all smile, the sun. We did it. Me and him. Him and me. Without shame. Our loveshipping. And then I told him all about Maristrela and Tila—and he didn't get jealous. "None of that exists: just you and me!" And he put on his cambric T-shirt and beige corduroys, and with arms slung over shoulders we went along the paths leading out of paradise—the angel with the sword didn't see us pass by.

With Sissy it was friendship without measure, the pure bliss of our pond under the naked moon. And the blind-souled bitch killed my most beautiful shooter, the marble with a sun spinning inside it, blond sparkles. The teacher hag called us fags.

So what's your verdict, man? I was friends with a woman, with Maristrela, never once laying hands on her tattered slip—ours was a love of friendship, with her homeliness and that gleam in her eyes. And I was the lover of a man, of Sissy—me and him, him and me, one. So what do you think? No opinion? Nothing? Honest, man, it's not that I want to flatter you, but I like your attitude, I do, I'd like to be like you. Not to speak about what you don't know—that's a wise wisdom.

By the law comes sin—I turn around the saying

of my father professor in seminary. And I wonder, off-side: sin, what is it? A crime? . . .

The morning star, tertiary—my two ladies, and him, my friend. The twinkle stops and out comes the Verdean, who at twelve years of age took up whoring for Katonho, a white-trash who didn't do anything right: he had the face of a crook and never cheated anyone; the voice of an opera singer and never once whistled; women cuddled up to him and he kept right on reading his books. How could he corrupt my sweetheart, just twelve, with just-sprouted nipples on her scrawny chest? I think she must have forced him to. . . .

At any rate, it's a sin, was a sin, prostitution. Shameless, brazen-faced harlotry, vying with rivals for the fat-cat clients. Dirty words in their mouths, wine in their bellies, purposely diseased and pretending they weren't, and the laughter of the eyes that poked knitting needles into the chirping birds: "This guy's all set! Won't he be surprised at what he got for his money!" All skin and bones, unsightly, miserable little demoness, her bugging eyes crowding out her she-rat snout. And then her hair grew out, without all the frizz, like a Verdean-Asian's, a gorgeous full head. Her ringworm scabs fell off. The flesh in her cheeks turned from pallid to rosy, rouged. Her thin chapped lips gave birth to moist soft-ness. And her body, the chalice of sin, covered with eczema and itching like an anthill, began to beautify. Her mulatto legs got long and her behind high, serene. Small breasts, the mere foam of waves, smiling. I never again said as much as good-day to her, I never saw her body without any clothes—the pure friendship of ugli-ness bowed out to prettiness. And her beauty grew along with her corruption: the more she fornicated, the prettier she got. And her little field-mice brothers stuffed their hungry tummies, they grew up in the shadow of bare-legged bank notes; Dona Catita got her first brand-new dress, never worn by another; and the family's father, alias the Cape Verdean, got a steady job working for a white man downtown. Family bliss, I remember, for as long as I stayed on in my shantytown. In vacations from seminary I'd see all the Cape Verdean's Verdean kids, some of them even wearing shoes, the thick kind that inmates from the Mpungu a Ndongo prison used to make. Life had given them its flowers, its fruits, the shade of the manioc tree on Sundays. Only in the manure of mortal sin was happiness born—is that how God wanted it?

I know, man, I know the evangelical answer: who gains the word loses his own soul, etc., etc.

Sorry, but that's scant water to satisfy my thirst. The sin of pride? See?! You never reach an end unless you never started. That's why I left seminary. I think only Father Viêra, father of my addiction to Latin high-talk, was sorry to see me go. But I raised too many questions, too many doubts. And whoever doubts—shut up or get out!

Is that what sin is—wanting to know, questioning to know?

I always question, even when I know, because I could be mistaken. . . .

Listen, man, to the scandalously absurd Greek term they stuck on me, sexopath, in Paragraph D. Is that a word for civilized people to use? Was I so bad that they have to label me with an obscenity to make your mouth drop? These bigwigs of justice, doctor prosecutors, and the whole shifty lot are all stone deaf. If I was a defense lawyer I'd only use beautiful words: if the crime wasn't ugly, the words would match; and if the crime was ugly, they'd help absolve human nature.

Words lie? You're a man with schooling, you know the right comebacks—did you study at a Jesuit seminary? Words lie, but people use them to tell the truth!

Sexopath? Preposterous!

Man, have you ever seen a woman naked and tattooed in her triangle of love? Ay! my Sodomy-Galores . . .

My Bailundo girl: I don't know if I should say anything. Will you understand my meaning? Not twist my thread? Comprehend, not condemn? That for me she is . . . the beauty of all that hairless skin, mocha chocolate. But how could I forget: you're a comrade pal of the sea, of land, and of air—boat, feet, and birds! So let's go. Do you see the sea in just one color? Does it have only the deep-blue color of its deep, or the yellow of the coast? Every fish has its own depth, every wave its particular foam, every sky its special shade. The sea is multiple, multifarious—it's beauty. And the colored flock of birds? Take the goldfinches, greenfinches, hummingbirds by the hundred, the bluebreasts—which of them is just one pure color, monotony? The common sparrow has more earth-brown hues than you can count! . . . And so a woman, loveliness of our rib reincarnate, would have to be just as breath-raking, no? I saw her unused teenage body and her taut skin, without any hair, and I rejoiced—the first and only pearl to turn up in my life. On the beaches of her body I traced flowers,

Cupid's arrows, my sweet nothings: lovely lover, beloved love. I filled the whole triangle of her Mesopotamia with gardens—blue flowers, fine and tiny, my paradise of Eden. I love love. I couldn't squander that body of hers so beautifully beautiful. I'm not an animal to just huff and puff, humping my butt up and down in bed. With me it's different, different every time—I correct life, I invent as I go. I come from people with class—yes, sir—a woman should be savored. Me a sexopath? You believe that, man? You don't? You're an honest soul, and sensitive—it comes through right away. We get on all right together.

I rotate my star: the center is one and always the same, the points are three, one star only but never equal. Florinha, forever. Prostibrute, half crazy—just listen and you'll see. She led a miserable life, slept with the dregs no other whore would have, and she didn't even care: she got by on a dollar or two. She did laundry for people from town: she'd wash their clothes, then wear, rewash, and deliver them.

She wasn't stingy: we ate up her money in candy. "Florinha, a quarter!" "Florinha, some peanuts!" The boar-sized spaces between her teeth would smile. "My children, children of my suffering . . . have all you want!" And the secret that was ours and that I spilled without meaning to . . . my grown-up pretensions, my revenge against the hysterical doctor that had kidnapped Tila from the orphanage. The ritual, top-secret secret: on the tenth of each month, early in the morning, a huge pot of black sugar brewing; a can with sand and salt, a skillet, the peanuts roasting. We looked on from a distance; we were forbidden, positively, to come close.

The shells would fly up high in the wind of her blowing, the swallows swooping down to snag them, looking like flying white ants from when after it rains. And then she'd scrub her washboard and put soap on the back so that the sugar wouldn't stick: wooden spoon, peanuts, and the poor-man's candies were born, a dark brown. The pieces dried under the manioc tree. Without sun, because the sun sucks out flavor. On that day she didn't receive clients, she'd yell insults to whoever propositioned her. At seven o'clock we were all quiet, waiting for the signal. Ginito, the other older kids, and me, with my eight years. The candle appeared in the window—time for our happy-birthday party. One at a time, cautious panthers, we crawled along through the grass to her yard. There we entered another world. Hell? Heaven? This is the story, man:

On the tenth day of a certain month Ninito died, he was killed. Ninito was her son, her sustenance. And she punctually celebrated his passing away, a poor-folks' Mass with the neighborhood boys. From among her bundled-up things she'd pull out his picture, smiling in overalls, and set it on the shelf with black crepe streamers, then light the candles. On the table there'd be fresh corn cider, and behind the jug the peanut candies she made. And she received us like a lady: high heels and a long dress. By the light from the photograph's candles, we could tell she was naked underneath. Ginito would laugh—he was twelve years old. We'd hold hands and sing our songs softly, in a whisper, the way she instructed. We'd drink and eat, she'd start turning around, dancing with her eyes closed, already in her trance, and Ninito would speak. She'd dance and dance, her dress lifting up, her skinny old legs showing as she twirled and rocked. The first one was Ginito, the oldest of us, almost a man. She'd take him behind the partitioning blanket: she'd laugh and laugh. "Not that way!" She taught him how. Ginito would come out all red in the face. We all waited our turn. She was the mother-of-love: she taught us what we still didn't need to know but were going to need. We were the friends of her passed-away son; she offered us her only and unique treasure. At first she wouldn't do it with me, I was small fry. At last came my first time—it wasn't long after I'd seen the world's first simian doctor, screeching on top of Tila. I blew it, I exposed her: there she was on the mat, so shriveled up that I felt sorry for her, I remembered the orphan girl I liked and the rangotang ape yelling at her—I plunged in. And I was mad. Florinha grabbed me by the shoulders and murmured: "Poor thing! Still a child . . . So little—where are you, little dicky?" I was raging mad: I was eight years old, with Tila I'd almost been married, and this woman had the nerve to make fun of me? I panted, I seethed, I remembered the ape man, I shimmied my bottom around, eyes closed. And she began to cry: "Why always me? Ay, my suffering, my life! Such a young thing, almost white, an almost white child, God my Father! . . ." She was being my mother, sad at what I'd just learned. I got even madder; I shouted, "Electricity!" I don't remember what else happened. They told me later that we fought, I ripped her clothes, bruised her, scratched with my nails, and howled like a madman, like one possessed. My claque, all together, sang a happy-birthday-to-you of "Electricity! Electricity!"

Everyone.

My father was the first one to arrive, yanking me from on top her. My witch of a stepmother gave one peek inside and then ran hollering all over the shantytown. Ginito's mother came, all the mothers, the stepmothers, and the mistresses, too, whether or not they had sons. A horrendous lynching: a hail of sticks and stones, Florinha smack in the middle of the street, defending herself by the light of the moon. The irate women were like bloodthirsty beasts: they yanked out hair, pulled at the prostitute's dried-out breasts, spat on her, scratched her. "The police! The police for this shameless slut!" "Corrupter of innocent boys, the temptress!" I don't have it in me to repeat all their curses. One thing I know: men don't have half the imagination for insulting!

Even my father gave up trying to save her. He gave me two good slaps, making me pay for his exasperation with the women, and hauled me home. I still remember Florinha with her hands tied behind her back, shoved along by the bitchy pack toward the police station—Miss Jesus on her way to Calvary. And Ginito's mother, a lady who never missed a Mass or procession, used a stick to lift the train of her skirt, tapping her on the butt and yelling, "March, hussy, march!" And all the women laughed.

They set her shack on fire, it burned clean down. They sent her off to the Tiger Bay prison. Sometimes my father, sitting by the door, would look at the burned ground and the ashen ruins, mumbling, and I'd hear, "Not even any panties, the brazen wench! Not even any panties . . ."

Women adore the children of everyone, so why, at

that moment, did they act like no one else had ever given birth? Is a mother's love exclusive hatred, the growling of a bitch with her bone?

I had many mothers and never knew my own. Florinha—I say that lovely name and see my mother, my unknown mother. Things I never saw but know, because they're known: black, short, a tribal chief's daughter—so I'm blue-blooded, but I don't strut. I'd hardly started crawling when they cast a spell on her for being hooked up with a Caucaphile. It was my father brought me out of the Golungo woods to this city on the edge of the sea.

I love Luanda, man—its houses, streets, trees, the sea, sky and clouds, the isthmus where fishermen fish. I never knock beauty, no matter what kind. I say "Luanda" and my heart smiles, my eyes close, I'm homesick. As I'm only really here when I'm far away. It's from far away that one loves. Because I don't like the people—a bunch of city-slick swine. The government ought to build settlements in the boondocks for all these idiots to go live in. Then all that would be left is the city's empty beauty—houses and trees and the rest. No one would spoil it anymore with their body odor. I don't get on with Luanda folk: be they white, be they black, be they mixed, I spit on them all. Petty-minded people with their petty town! Haven't they ever heard of New York, Nagasaki? Imperial Rome, Scandinavia? Uncouth sons of beetles!

You chuckle, do you, at my thirst for pretty things? I met one guy—gracious!: "From being a tribal doctor in the woods I moved up to being a delivery man in Luanda," boasted the proud fool.

Sorry! I was breaking the thread—the beads were

scattering, setting us back. It's been a long time since I been with a man like you to orchestrate the colors. With me it's been a poor slave mixture; with you it's emancipated beauty. I think of Sissy, I see him smiling. But Sissy . . . Sissy was . . . and he isn't anymore.

The only one that, when I say friend, makes my heart heavy, and I feel a soft sorrow.

I was the only one allowed in, alone I went in, wearing the shoes he'd given me. The others, outside. A private room—all white, and him too. White, white, white, and his widowed mother dressed in black, Holy Cross in her hands. He never opened his eyes again; I took his warm hand, my tears started falling, and he smiled. "Juju!"—a bird's light breath. His mama put her finger to her lips, for silence. I stayed until five o'clock, my hand in his, telling him jokes as our friendship love whirred round and round—he died the next day. Our executioner teacher was booted out—transferred. It all started the day my father went ahead and bought me a sisal sack with a cartoon character. I'd had my heart set on it for a long time. I was ashamed of the old denim one hanging on the wall. Birds fluttered inside me when I woke up next morning: we were going to skip school, me and Sissy, I'd show him the cartooned sack. We would go to the ocean, we were going to go, but my stepmother jinxed everything. She gave me a new writing slate and pencil and pulled my ears: "I'll break your head open if you ruin this one. . . ." And so I didn't meet up with Sissy, he was already in school, no way we could skip. I took his hand, tugged him into a corner, and showed him my sack. He looked into my eyes, the yellow sack made of sisal, with the blue-green-purple-black cartoon of a boy with his dog, books, and homework: "I like you!" And we kissed, our secret. The executioner teacher hag caught us—she and an assistant—and dragged us off to the bathroom. The blood of my friend won't ever leave my hands—I was too late in shielding his body. His lungs were weak, he'd had TB when he was little. "Queers"—and the blind-souled bitch thrashed, and the baboon assistant thrashed. . . .

It makes me cry, man. I'll nevermore again in my life be happy—I don't have it in me to tell the rest. It's just silence: he died. The beautifulest corpse I've seen to this day: blond, white, fresh, without one red stain of blood beneath his skin. I kissed him in his coffin—my friend to dust, utter dust. . . .

Where was I? Am I back in the Sala-Kabanga woods, far away from Golungo, far away from Cerca?

You're considerate, man, you really are: you respected my sorrow, you hushed and didn't interrupt the flow. Thank you, my friend, thank you. Now I can stop questioning—I have the evidence of your testimony: pure loveship it was and can never again be. Pure beauty—it returns, I overcome Sissy's death, he lives with me in my eyes' pupils. If I see blue, it's him; if sea-green, it's him; if I find something lovely, he is with me. Always. My Bailundo girl . . .

Does death exist? You and your crazy questions, man! . . . Death? What's that? A dread not worth a dime! Lady Death belongs to a fantastic fable—she doesn't exist. We can't explain, explicate, define, or describe her, so how can we pretend she's actual, factual? There are no words for her. . . . Words lie, you say?

You're clever with your comebacks! "Open your eyes, Juvêncio, you're in Luanda. . . ." They lie, yes, they lie; but they're the mother of truth, they truly are. . . . Here's what I think: one day, when someone visits the heavenly angels or brimstone devils and returns to tell the journey, a sailor that sails away and comes back in May, then—yes, sir—death will exist!

What no one's yet told doesn't yet exist. All there is is our dreaded dumb ignorance! Man still hasn't discovered death. If we still haven't reached the moon, something seeable, how much less . . . .

I get along with death, I said so and don't take it back. The fabled Lady doesn't scare me. My only fear is the one I've told you—the absence of voices, faces and human hearts, the deserted desert, solitary solitude. I sometimes even sleep with the light on, to make believe there's sun in my room. Darkness is harmful to the heart. In the darkness of solitude he's always there, which I wasn't going to tell you, man, because I can't find the answer. The question is: to alleviate pain, can one kill, in cold blood? Ninito, Florinda's son, an apprentice mechanic, his household's sustenance. He wasn't like the rest of us. He was older and more serious, less silly, less delirious—not just another naughty brat. "Hard work set him right early on!" pronounced Florinda. Because she was sorry he didn't play with us? And therefore boasting of her grown-up son, man of the house, when he was still only a teen? She said—we heard her—that every weekend he brought home every penny of his pay. Where will I get the courage to tell you the odious death of that poor soul! . . .

Are you a Bible man, have you read the Holy Writ?

You know the pock-eclipse of Saint John, the part that comes after the Epistles, in the New Testament of Our Lord Jesus Christ? Can you hear in your ears the trumpets of the seven angels—man chasing death, death fleeing? The multiheaded red dragon, the beasts descending from the air, rising from land and sea, covered with horns? Babylonia the whore, seated in the sewer waters, swigging her abominations from the golden chalice? All of this that your memory reinvents is nothing, man, just a cricket's piss, compared with Ninito, stark naked, in an iron cage, digging his teeth into the bars and howling, his body transfigured into that of a Chinese circus ape—Lord God forgive me. . . .

It was just a dog. A tiny little mutt that didn't even stop by his door or anything. He was sitting there, six o'clock, on break from his Sunday labor, some odd job or other. He whistled, the dog snarled, uninterested. He laughed, tried to grab hold—a small awkward bite, nothing at all, he shook off the dog, which trotted away, and took a nap. The next Sunday he couldn't so much as wash himself or drink water, it was terrible.

He fled, we fled. . . .

They shooed us out of Charity Hospital, where he could be heard howling from far away. Nothing they could do. Two vaccinated attendants could no longer hold him down. He ran naked through the aisles of the wards, hobbling as he went, baring his fangs and drooling all over the patients. He was a beast on the loose, ranting and ravaging. They nabbed him with a net and put him in the municipal truck, like as if he was a stray dog. I saw five hefty men on top who couldn't hold him down; he shook them off and shredded the net. General panic and flight. We climbed into the trees, Florinha cried in the street, in the middle of the street. They clubbed him and he screeched like a chimpanzee mother robbed of her chimp babies. They put him in a cage with iron bars. Padlocked. Naked, his privates dangling, his body all swelled. There was no one could help him anymore, they dragged Florinha away in the police car. "My son! My son!" In the distance we could still hear her wails, in between his monkey screeches. His teeth shattering against the iron bars, his mouth all blood, his fingernails, too. He started ripping his own flesh, tearing off pieces with his nails and eating it. Devouring it! He was no longer a human. A cannibal ape—why did they let him suffer, the sadists? From the top of the tall acacia, in our deathly frightened silence, we saw the doctor with his attendants, talking and gesticulizing. The screaming screeching shrieks of Ninito, raging. His arms were a mass of blood. He no longer saw, just chewed. An attendant went up to the cage to distract him, so that the doctor could put him to sleep with a shot. "They're going to do him in!" said Ginito. I looked at the son of the God-fearing woman and smiled: "Ninito died a long time ago. What we see there is a chimpanzee!" But the syringe never touched him, it was all a tinkling of glass, the doctor jumping back for his life.

I'm almost through, man. They fetched a pistol, with the police chief looking on, and the hospital employees there as witnesses, the doctor fired, his soul departed, we saw it go up in the smoke.

It was five-thirty, I remember the time because of the train whistle in the distance. "They 'sassinated him,"

Ginito said as he began to climb down out of the tree. But I took issue: "Ninito died at home. That creature there was a little gorilla," I explained. I was a simpleton in those days.

Nowadays?

Why did he, Ninito, a good person and hardworking, have to die in such a bad way? Sins? He was just a kid! And later on I also began to wonder: is it all right to kill, if it's to bring peaceful relief? His mother said do it, but does Our Lord go along?

God oh God, the fears, the dreads! Even if he did change, transformed into the animal before evolution, what about his soul? Only when the body's dead does the soul depart—was his soul transformed, too? Is there some reason why Ninito, our constant good example at home, had to descend from such a bright destiny to such a bleak one, without guilt, judgment, or the chance of purgatory?

I know you can't lead me out of this forest, man. Even Reverend Father Viêra, with his clever dog-Latin, never could give me a good answer—I left him pondering my stories when I took off. . . .

But in the dark of my solitude I sometimes grumble that God isn't fair—death should be equal for all!

I see, man, what you're seeing. . . . The pale greens of the rustling Indian fig leaves. The hundred-color parakeets that come from Roçadas—they belong to the prison guards—their beauty flitting about the grounds, carefree. Railroad is what they call that guy over there shaving his beard, patting his cheeks—his fiancée's coming to visit and he wants to look smart! And that blue sky without a patch of cloud, and the ocean on the far side of that farthest house, I wish I could see it. And us two sitting here, our friendly banter. It's already past three—my Bailundo girl will be here soon with her famous goodies, Moamba stew with that golden sauce, a specialty in the south, in the Benguela-Catumbela lands. I'm being Sissy right now—you're to blame for my pupils raining alleluias again.

I'm an ingenerate malefactor. . . .

A hopeless, confirmed delinquent, sentenced for indefinitely: homicide, sado-heresy, enslavement. . . .

Here she comes, my southland sweetheart. Her smile, life. Gleaming gem, my fine silver . . . Mwenge wange, my life, yes . . . I'm going to hang a surprise on her—the chain of slavery: the necklace of your multiple colors. . . .

This man ask the craziest questions! . . . Separate beads on the string—you think that's what a man's life is? Red beads, blue beads, this color, that color, all in a row? No, sir! . . . Everything a man does is all of him, whole—each and every color is the rainbow.

(June 27 to July 1, 1968)